Clifford's
Busy Week

For Drew, Emily, and Carly
—N.B.

The author thanks Manny Campana and Grace Maccarone
for their contributions to this book.

ISBN 978-0-545-22312-6

12 11 10 9 8 7 6 5 4   10 11 12 13 14

Printed in the U.S.A.   40
This edition first printing, May 2010

Clifford's
Busy Week

SCHOLASTIC READER
LEVEL 1
50-250 WORDS

Norman Bridwell

Cartwheel
·B·O·O·K·S·®

SCHOLASTIC INC.
New York   Toronto   London   Auckland
Sydney   Mexico City   New Delhi   Hong Kong

Clifford loves his toy mouse.

But where is it?

It is not in the doghouse.

It is not in the people house.

Clifford wants to find his toy.
He will look for it every day this week.

On Sunday, Clifford goes
to the playground.

The toy mouse is not there.

It is not there.

On Monday, Clifford goes
to the market.

His toy is not there.

Clifford is crying.

On Tuesday, Clifford goes
to the fun park.

The toy mouse is not on the ride.

It is not in the fun house.

It is not at the game.

On Wednesday, Clifford goes
to the farm.

His toy mouse is not in the barn.

His toy mouse is not with the chickens.
Ah-choo! Feathers make Clifford sneeze.

On Thursday, Clifford goes to the gym.

His toy is not there.

On Friday, Clifford goes to the lake.

The toy mouse is not in the boats.

It is not under the boats.

Dad gives Clifford a new toy mouse.
Clifford does not want it.

On Saturday, Dad plays golf.
Is the toy mouse in the hole?

Clifford digs and digs.

His mouse is not there.

Later, Clifford goes to Grandma's house.
He is very sad.

"Here is your mouse," says Grandma.
"You left it here last week."

Clifford thanks Grandma.
He is happy now!